**JEREMY STRONG** once worked in a bakery, putting the jam into three thousand doughnuts every night. Now he puts the jam in stories instead, which he finds much more exciting. At the age of three, he fell out of a first-floor bedroom window and landed on his head. His mother says that this damaged him for the rest of his life and refuses to take any responsibility. He loves writing stories because he says it is 'the only time you alone have complete control and can make anything happen'. His ambition is to make you laugh (or at least snuffle). Jeremy Strong lives near Bath with his wife, Gillie, four cats and a flying cow.

## ARE YOU FEELING SILLY ENOUGH TO READ MORE?

LAUGH YOUR SOCKS OFF WITH

# JEREMY STRONG

## CARTOON KID EMERGENCY!

ILLUSTRATED BY

## STEVE MAY

PUFFIN

# PUFFIN BOOKS

Published by the Penguin Group
Penguin Books Ltd, 80 Strand, London WC2R 0RL, England
Penguin Group (USA) Inc., 375 Hudson Street, New York, New York 10014, USA
Penguin Group (Canada), 90 Eglinton Avenue East, Suite 700, Toronto, Ontario, Canada M4P 2Y3
(a division of Pearson Penguin Canada Inc.)
Penguin Ireland, 25 St Stephen's Green, Dublin 2, Ireland (a division of Penguin Books Ltd)
Penguin Group (Australia), 250 Camberwell Road, Camberwell, Victoria 3124, Australia
(a division of Pearson Australia Group Pty Ltd)
Penguin Books India Pvt Ltd, 11 Community Centre, Panchsheel Park, New Delhi – 110 017, India
Penguin Group (NZ), 67 Apollo Drive, Rosedale, North Shore 0632, New Zealand
(a division of Pearson New Zealand Ltd)
Penguin Books (South Africa) (Pty) Ltd, 24 Sturdee Avenue, Rosebank, Johannesburg 2196, South Africa

Penguin Books Ltd, Registered Offices: 80 Strand, London WC2R 0RL, England

puffinbooks.com

First published 2012
001 – 10 9 8 7 6 5 4 3 2 1

Text copyright © Jeremy Strong, 2012
Illustrations copyright © Steve May, 2012
All rights reserved

The moral right of the author and illustrator has been asserted

Set in Baskerville
Made and printed in England by Clays Ltd, St Ives plc

British Library Cataloguing in Publication Data
A CIP catalogue record for this book is available from the British Library

ISBN: 978–0–141–33995–5

www.greenpenguin.co.uk

MIX
Paper from
responsible sources
FSC™ C018179

Penguin Books is committed to a sustainable
future for our business, our readers and our
planet. This book is made from paper certified
by the Forest Stewardship Council.

*This is for two REAL superstars,
my grandchildren, Sam and Ben.*

# CONTENTS

# VAMPIRE ROBBERS

# KRRRRRNK!

# SKWKKKK!

## DRRRRRRSKWK!

That's the noise the packed-lunch trolley makes when it's being pushed from our classroom and across the hall to the dining area. The **_BRRAANNG!!_** bit is when it crashes into the school piano halfway there. The trolley always crashes into the piano because it's got a wonky wheel. It's also got

another wheel that keeps sticking and goes
***whizz whizz whrrrr SPLRRRRR!*** and
grinds to a halt.

That packed-lunch trolley is in a bad way,
if you ask me. Someone should take it to
the Trolley Hospital. It probably needs an
operation.

HMMM, I CAN SEE
CLOGGED COGS. THIS
PATIENT NEEDS A
WHEEL BYPASS.

Nobody in our class likes pushing that trolley. When I say 'nobody', I mean nobody except Hartley Tartly-Green. Hartley is such a goody-goody he'd throw himself off a cliff if a teacher asked him to.

Most of us in our class have a packed lunch. This is what some of us get.

I'M A GOOD BOY! OW!

My lunch box.

Pete's lunch box.

SURPRISE!

Mr Butternut's lunch box.

Mia's lunch box.

Sarah Sitterbout's lunch box.

Hartley Tartly-Green's lunch box.

Tyson's lunch box.

Cameron's lunch box.

As you can see, Pete's hamster, Betty, is in his lunch box. Betty has eaten half his sandwiches too. Pete often finds her in strange places because she's always escaping. Pete's swimming trunks have also escaped – from his legs and into his lunch box. They'd been missing for days before they turned up here. Pete's like that, which is why I call him Super Conk. (And many other things.)

Pete is my best friend. He has a BIG
NOSE and the most ENORMOUS feet.
They are even bigger than the *Titanic*!
(And they don't float either.)

I've got a pet too. His name is Colin and he is EXOTIC. *Exotic* means unusual and strange. Colin is a chameleon and his tongue is longer than my ruler, which definitely makes him VERY strange.

*I can lick stamps in one go!*

Did you see what Mr Butternut has in *his* lunch box? Champagne! That's because teachers drink champagne ALL the time, AND they eat strawberries and cream. They keep it all in the staffroom. You know those big water coolers you can get a drink of water from? Well, the teachers have one of those, only it's full of champagne. IT'S TRUE! You ask one. (Dare you!)

Mr Butternut is our class teacher and he is the coolest teacher in the universe. Well, most of the time. Sometimes he gets cross and then I don't call him Mr Butternut. I call him Mr Horrible Hairy Face because he's got a beard. Mr Butternut says we are all superheroes and can do ANYTHING.

Actually, I don't think Mr Butternut really means that. I mean, we can't do ANYTHING, can we? For starters, we can't tie Miss Scratchitt, our head teacher, to a post and bombard her with giant tomatoes.

SPLURRP!

IF YOU STOP, YOU CAN HAVE ALL MY CHAMPAGNE!

GIANT TOMATO FIRING CANNON

CARTOON KID!

BIG FEET PETE!

CURLY WURLY GIRL!

BIG BUM BRAIN!

We've got superhero names too. I'm Cartoon Kid because I'm always drawing stuff. Pete is Big Feet Pete, of course. Mia is Curly-Wurly-Girly because of her hair. And Sarah Sitterbout is Big Bum Brain because she's got a big bum AND a big brain. She is cleverer than the fattest encyclopedia in the library and knows EVERYTHING. She's got so much brain inside her head I'm surprised it's not falling out of her ears.

Anyhow, most of us have a packed lunch and this is the noise you hear in the lunch hall when we are all eating:

# SHLIPPP
# SQUIRRRCH
# NGG-NGG-NGGULP!

Mr Butternut says it sounds like feeding time at the zoo. That's silly because most of the teachers eat in the lunch hall and that means they must be animals too. Pete and I have a great game where we watch the teachers eating and guess what animal they would be.

So, just before lunch, two of us have to push the trolley across to the lunch hall. Yesterday it was the turn of Erin and Hartley Tartly-Green. Erin has only just moved to our school. She wears a nest on her head. Erin says it's her hair, but I reckon

it looks more
like a pair of
crows have been
knitting cardigans
from her hair –
and, as you know,
crows aren't any
good at knitting.
Obviously.

Erin wears
socks that don't
match and fastens
her buttons
in the wrong
buttonholes. She
likes drawing

**HMMMMMM!**

(like me!), sticks out her tongue when she's concentrating and hums. Hummm, hhhmmm, mmmmm —

like that. Sometimes she sucks the end of her felt tips and ends up with assorted colours all round her mouth, like a rainbow has just crashed into her face. Also, she's always dropping things. Apart from that, she's quite normal.

So, Erin and Hartley T-G had to take the lunch trolley across to the dining area. To do that, you go through our cloakroom and next-door's cloakroom. This is always difficult because of the wonky wheel and the sticky wheel. The trolley crashes into everything.

Erin and Hartley Tartly were squeaking and grinding their way through the next-door cloakroom when they got a nasty surprise.

# THEY WERE AMBUSHED!

By the time they were discovered, all tied
up and nowhere to go, it was too late. The
lunch boxes had been opened and all the
yummiest bits had gone.

Mr Horrible Hairy Face was
VERY cross. (Probably because his
champagne had been stolen.) He
looked at us grimly.

Trap them!

'We must catch the packed-lunch
robbers,' he announced.

Good idea. But how?

Tyson waved his arm around like
a flag. 'Why don't we mount some
machine guns on the trolley, and when
the robbers jump out we can go *dugga-
dugga-dugga-dugga-dugga* and shoot them?
Or hide a python in Hartley's lunch
box, and when the robbers open it the
snake jumps out, squeezes them to
death and eats them?'

'I don't want a python in my lunch box,'
complained Hartley Tartly. 'It's new, and it's
got Thomas the Tank Engine on it.'

Mr Butternut rubbed his beard. 'We do not
shoot people or put snakes in lunch boxes,
Tyson,' he explained. 'We have a big problem.
I will sleep on it.'

What? Why would our teacher want to sleep on a problem? Why not sleep on a bed?

I wouldn't sleep on a problem if you paid me.

We all looked at each other and scratched our heads until Sarah Sitterbout explained (because she knows so much).

'Mr Butternut means he's going to think about it while he's asleep,' she told us.

'How can you think when you're asleep?' demanded Hartley Tartly. 'That's very silly.'

I told you. Trap them!

'Hartley, you can't even think when you're awake,' Cameron pointed out, and everyone fell about.

We all tried to think of how to catch the robbers, but it was no good.

It got to the end of the afternoon and Mr Butternut read us a story. He always reads to us every day, and it's often the best time we have. Last week he told us a really cool story called 'The Wooden Horse of Troy'. It was so exciting our mouths were open the WHOLE time. (Hartley was dribbling!)

# SARAH SITTERBOUT'S BIT ABOUT THE TROJAN HORSE

The Ancient Greeks were at war with the Trojans at Troy. The Greeks couldn't get into the city, so they pretended to go away, leaving behind a gift for the Trojans - a giant wooden horse. In fact, the Greeks had hidden their soldiers inside the horse. The Trojans thought the wooden horse was wonderful and pulled the statue inside the city walls. (Q. Was that stupid, or what? A. Yes, it was.) That night, the Greeks jumped out of the horse and the Trojans were defeated. I bet it was really smelly with all those soldiers stuck inside that horse. Urrgh!

POO! YOU PONG!

FARP!

YOU'RE A BIGGER PONG THAN ME!

That night we all tried to sleep on our problems like Mr Butternut said he was going to. Pete's problem turned out to be Betty the hamster. She'd escaped again and was hiding in his bed. My problem was my big sis, Abbie, who started snoring at one o'clock in the morning.

The next day we trooped into school and found Mr Butternut sitting on the edge of his desk waving his feet about and wearing a big grin. (I don't mean his feet were wearing the big grin – it was on his face.)

'Last night I had an idea of how to catch the lunch-box robbers, but I need your help,' he explained. 'I have thought of a way to trap them!'

That's what I said! Trap them!

'Two or three of you are small enough to hide inside the trolley beneath some of the lunch boxes. When the trolley gets attacked, you all leap out. There would be enough of you to frighten the robbers, and we will hear your cries and come dashing out to help. Then we shall see who the robbers are at last!'

What a brilliant plan! That Mr Butternut is mighty clever, if you ask me. It must be all that champagne.

Sarah Sitterbout got very excited.

IT'S JUST LIKE THE TROJAN HORSE.

She was right too! Of course she was. Sarah Sitterbout is always right. We all knew the story. We had even drawn pictures of it and mine was one of the best. That's what Mr Butternut said.

Pete said the only reason I could draw horses was because I was one. 'You are a small, ginger, knobbly-kneed horse-twit,' he said, using those exact words.

CASPER'S
IS THE
BEST !

'And your feet are submarines and your face is a secret submarine base and your nose is another submarine coming out of it,' I told him, using those exact words.

Then we hit each other a few times because we are best friends.

'We're going to have a Trojan Trolley!' shouted Cameron. 'Fantastic!'

'I don't want to hide in a trolley,' murmured Tyson, who is frightened of everything, even his own teeth.

'I'll go in the trolley!' Mia volunteered.

'So will I!' Pete immediately shouted. Do you know why he said that? Because Pete LOVES Mia! Mmmm, he does. Poor Pete's in love! Mia has got freckles and masses of curly hair, which she hates. We call her Curly-Wurly-Girly.

'Casper, how about you?' asked Mr Butternut. 'There's still room for a smallish person.'

Poor Pete wants to be on his own with Mia!

Pete was madly shaking his head as if he had an owl stuck up his nose. (That's how big his nose is!) 'No, no, no, no, no, no, no room, no room for smallish people, not even ginger twiglet-type persons,' he claimed.

Mr Butternut ignored him and grinned at us. 'The more people we can hide in the trolley, the better. Those pesky lunch robbers are going to get a big surprise!'

So that was decided. Cameron and Sarah offered to push the trolley, and Pete, Mia and I clambered into it and had lunch boxes piled on top of us.

Off we went –

# KRRRRRNK! SKWKKKK! BRRAANNG! DRRRRRRSKWK!

– bashing into the school piano on the way, as usual. I can tell you, it was a bumpy ride. It was pretty annoying too, because of Pete's feet. They went everywhere, including in my ear. Twice. Meanwhile Pete sat there and gazed at Mia as if she was one big strawberry and vanilla ice cream. Mia pretended not to notice, but even her hair blushed.

I was just about to poke Pete – because when you're stuck in a trolley, all cramped

34

up, you have to do SOMETHING; anyhow,
I was just about to poke him when an
earthquake began. So did the screaming.

GRRR!
GOT YOU!

AAARGH!

And then the lunch trolley EXPLODED!

Well, obviously, it didn't *actually* explode.
What happened was that Pete and
Mia and I leaped OUT of the
trolley, and all the lunch boxes

YOU'RE HISTORY!
SNARRLL!

went flying up in

HELP!

the air and came clattering

down all over the place.

# BLOPP! SPLUPP! GLOOPP! SPLLLRGH!

The three of us landed on our feet and shouted 'HA!' like the International Kung Fu Champions we weren't and came face to face with Cameron and Sarah. Except that

KAPOW!

HA-YA!

Cameron and Sarah's faces weren't there any more because the robbers had bundled coats over them so they couldn't see. Now the robbers were busily tying them up with skipping ropes.

And the robbers were – THE VAMPIRE TWINS!

Yes. It was Gory and Tory. I might have known. They're always up to no good. They are BIG trouble too, and DANGEROUS. Mia and Pete and I looked at each other anxiously because now we had a *BIG PROBLEMO!*

There were only three of us, not five, as Mr Butternut had planned. Our brilliant teacher hadn't realized that Cameron and Sarah would be tied up and wouldn't be able to help.

There was only one thing to do. The three of us held hands, closed our eyes and yelled:

In fact, Pete and Mia and I stood there like lemons, staring at Gory and Tory while they got on with ransacking the lunch boxes. Fortunately, we must have been heard back in the classroom because all of a sudden a whirling

figure came crashing through the cloakroom.
It was the new girl, Erin. She was waving
her arms like windmills and screaming at the
Vampire Twins.

She hurled herself at the twins. They
staggered back in surprise, and Pete and I

DON'T YOU DARE
TOUCH MY EGG AND BANANA
SANDWICHES, YOU POXY
PACKED-LUNCH PINCHERS!

quickly rushed in to help. Behind us the rest of the class came pouring out, and next-door's class.

In a few seconds the Vampire Twins were surrounded. They sat on the floor in the midst of a pile of squashed food, looking very sorry for themselves. The head teacher, Miss Scratchitt, was sent for.

I THINK I'M SITTING ON A SQUASHED TOMATO.

I must say that we were all pretty impressed with Erin. She had saved the day. Who'd have thought someone so messy could do that? Mind you, I'm a bit worried about Erin's lunch. Egg and banana? What kind of sandwich is that? A very strange one, if you ask me.

Miss Scratchitt was HUGELY cross with the Vampire Twins. Well, you know how cross head teachers can get. It's a lot crosser than your class teacher. That's why they get paid more.

Did you know that before a teacher becomes a head, he or she has to go and have Cross lessons? Well, they do. They have Cross lessons in a special soundproof building hidden away at the bottom of a big council office. They have to roar as loudly as they can until flames come shooting out of their mouths. Then they get a certificate that says:

**CONGRATULATIONS! NOW YOU CAN BE A HEAD TEACHER!**

So the Vampire Twins stood there while Miss Scratchitt shouted at them until their ears were burned right off. (Just joking!) Then she made them clear up **THE WHOLE LOT.** Plus, for all the rest of the month, Gory and Tory had to serve US at lunchtime!

It was brilliant! They had to wear frilly little aprons and bring us our food and ask us what we wanted very politely, and they had to be NICE to everyone.

Wasn't that good? Yes, it was!

But I'm still not at all sure about those egg and banana sandwiches of Erin's. Or the crows on top of her head.

If I was a vampire chameleon, I'd suck flies. Yum!

# FAIRIES

That's the noise I make when I fall out of bed. Which I do quite often. I am also very good at falling off chairs, benches, walls and anything I happen to be sitting or lying on.

I DON'T DO IT ON PURPOSE! I am not Mr Stupido! Falling off things just sort of happens to me.

'One day, Casper,' my dad said, 'I am going to put glue on your pyjamas. That should keep you in bed.'

'But then I shan't be able to go to school,' I cheerfully pointed out.

Dad didn't have an answer to that! Ha ha!

Casper thinks
he's clever –
and he is!

52

What happened was, I had a nightmare. I was run over by a police car full of elephants. (They were police elephants, of course – two in the back and two in the front.) I was lying on the road and lots of little animals came hurrying out to help – hamsters and guinea pigs and mice – and they were all made from Lego. The animals quickly built a stretcher and an operating table, from Lego, of course. They lifted me on to the table. (Obviously, I was tiny too.) Then the surgeon came in and he was a big tortoise. Made from Lego.

And that was when I went

# 'OoOoOoOo!
# ARRRGGH!'
# KERRSPLUD!

Then I woke up and wondered what I was doing on my bedroom floor. My big sis, Abbie, came bursting in.

'I thought you'd died,' she grunted, sounding VERY disappointed because, obviously, I hadn't.

I love my big sis. She's so nice. NOT.
We're always quarrelling and calling each
other names. Here are two of my favourite
names for her: FATBUM and SNOT-
FACTORY. But the one I like best is

GROTTY-BOTTY-POTTY-FACE. I can't tell you what Abbie calls me because it is too RUDE. That big sis of mine is Bad News.

GROTTY-BOTTY-POTTY-FACE

I draw pictures of her too, as you can see. At school I sit next to my best friend, Pete. He's tall and he's got feet the size of skateboards. I call him Big Feet Pete. That's his superhero name. He has a big nose too. Anyhow, not only does Pete sit next to me, he lives right next door to me too.

I don't know why Pete bothers to live next door because he spends most of his time in MY house. That's because Pete's dad left three years back and now his mum has got a boyfriend called Uncle Boring. That's not his real name, though it should be. He's always telling you incredibly DULL things that you don't want to know. Uncle Boring's real name is Derek and he looks like this.

I'm a superhero. Call me Super Tongue!

ALWAYS BRUSH YOUR TEETH
UP, DOWN AND SIDEWAYS.
BLAH BORING BLAH.

Uncle Boring isn't
even an uncle either.
It's what Pete's mum
says he should call him.
Pete says Uncle Boring
is even less interesting
than a fly having a sleep,
so he comes round to my
house instead.

'Because your house is exciting,' he told me.

'Really? How come?'

'Because you've got the most incredibly
knobbly knees I have ever seen AND a pet
chameleon with a ginormous tongue. Plus,

your mum makes great cakes. My mum's cakes

are like rocks. You could sink a ship with my

mum's cakes.'

It's true. My mum makes brilliant cakes.

It's her business. She makes them for loads of

people – for birthdays and special occasions

and so on.

Anyhow, Pete and I always walk
home together – because, like I said,
we live next door, so we have to.
Sometimes we are dreadfully unlucky
and find ourselves walking home at
the same time as Abbie and her best
friend, Shashi. Shashi has got

very long, straight black hair
that's always glossy and looks as
if she polishes it every night with
hair polish. (Unlike Abbie's hair,
which is blonde and looks like custard
dribbling down her face.)

So Pete and I were walking home
and I was telling him about my
nightmare and who did we see up

ahead of us? Abbie. She was walking with someone, and guess what? It wasn't Shashi.

IT WAS A BOY!

I almost died laughing, and Pete looked like a sour lemon. His face was all scrunched up and his eyes were bulging fit to go *POP!* right out of his face.

'Urrrggghhh!' moaned Pete. 'They're holding hands! Yuck yuck yuck yuck yuck!'

'I bet that's the new boy in her class,' I said. 'She keeps going on about him at home. Ha ha, Abbie's got a BOYFRIEND!'

'Let's follow them!' whispered Pete.

'We are following them,' I said. 'They're going the same way as us.'

YEAH, BUT SHE'S GOING TO YOUR HOUSE!

MAYBE THAT'S BECAUSE SHE LIVES THERE.

We hung back a bit while Abbie and the new boy went into my house. We didn't want to be spotted. I felt as if I was a private detective investigating a deeply disturbing mystery – 'The Extraordinary Case of the Boy who Actually Liked Grotty-Botty-Potty-Face'.

I gave Pete a big grin. 'I think we had better go in and see what's going on.'

'Gotta change out of this pesky uniform first,' muttered Pete, nipping up to his front door. 'Otherwise Uncle Boring will go on at me for entire centuries. **BLAH BLAH BLAH BLAAAARGH!** See you in two seconds. Don't want to miss anything!'

'I'm going to change too,' I told him.

I went indoors and there was Mum
talking to Abbie and the new boy from her
school. (Abbie's fourteen and goes to the
Even Bigger School, for Even Bigger Twits.)
It turned out he was called Charlie. He was
speaking to Mum while Abbie gazed at him
with adoring eyes.

Me? A doctor?! I was still trying to recover from Mum's bombshell when Pete slipped through the front door. I hurriedly dragged him up to my room while I changed clothes.

'Pete, big problemo! Mum says she wants me to be an important doctor!'

'Good idea.' The idiot was actually grinning. He obviously didn't understand.

'But you have to look in people's ears and examine pimples on their bottoms,' I complained. 'It's not nice.'

'Just keep your eyes closed,' suggested Pete.

That friend of mine is a complete noodle brain, if you ask me. I was just about to suggest he went to hospital for a brain scan because he obviously didn't have one in his

head and maybe it was in his little toe when
we heard footsteps on the stairs.

'Abbie and Charlie are coming!' he
whispered, eyes bulging.

'I bet they're going to have a snog,' I
sniggered. 'Let's go and spy on them.'

We crept out of my room and crawled
along the hall on our bellies until we were
lying right outside Abbie's door.

The door suddenly opened and
Abbie was there, very annoyed, as
usual.

'Are you spying on us?'

'No.'

'Then why were you staring into
my keyhole?'

'Because I saw a spider run
in there and I didn't want you
to get scared because I know you're
frightened of very small creatures.'

Abbie folded her arms across her chest and looked at me stonily for a few seconds before shouting downstairs.

'MUM! Casper and Pete are spying on me and Charlie!'

Mum's voice came floating back up the stairs.

FAIRY WINGS

TRAMPOLINE

'Casper! Pete! Leave them alone. Come downstairs and go and play outside.'

So that smashed up our little bit of fun. Huh! Some people just want to spoil everything. Pete and I went trailing out into the back garden. And guess what I saw!

Abbie and Shashi must have been playing fairies on the trampoline. They're always dressing up as fairies. Dad says they're going through a 'Fairy Phase'.

*Uh-oh. I think Casper's getting an idea!*

I think they're going through a 'Stupid Phase' and it's lasted ever since they were born. I turned to my best friend.

'Pete,' I began, because that's his name. 'You see that window up there? That's Abbie's bedroom.'

'Gosh. That is so exciting, my little ginger twiglet.'

'You don't *sound* very excited,' I told him.

'Because I'm not,' he answered. 'Why are you telling me boring stuff about the windows in your house? I'm not the window cleaner.'

'Because, Very Annoying Person With Feet The Size Of Australia, if we jump high enough on the trampoline, we might be able to see through her window and catch them snogging!'

'Aha – good one, Little Knobbly Knees!' Pete's eyes lit up. 'And if we put on these fairy wings, we can bounce even higher!'

LOOK WHAT I CAN DO, WINKY-WONK!

BOYOINNG!

BOINNG!

We clambered on to the trampoline and slipped the fairy wings on to our backs. We looked at each other and collapsed in giggles. 'Hello, Very Tall Fairy,' I piped. 'My name is Plinky-Plonk. Who are you?'

'I'm Winky-Wonk,' squeaked Pete. 'Shall we go bouncy-wouncy, Plinky-Plonk?'

'Ooh, yes, let's!'

And we did.

BET YOU CAN'T DO THIS, PLINKY-PLONK!

Higher and higher we went. I had to twist round to get a glimpse inside Abbie's room. And that's when the two fairies collided at high altitude. Our heads came crashing together.

THUDDUNK!

BUDUMM!

OWW!

It was REALLY REALLY PAINFUL! We plunged back on to the trampoline, clutching our foreheads and moaning. I took my hand away from my head and looked at it.

BLOOD!

Pete was bleeding too.

MUCHO PROBLEMO!

I said there'd be trouble.

'Mum! Dad!'

Dad came rushing out and found us sitting in the middle of the trampoline, holding our heads and with blood on our faces.

'Let me see those cuts,' said Dad. He took one look and uttered the fatal word: 'Hospital. Come on, into the car, both of you.' He clapped a hand to his own forehead. 'You would do this when your mother's just gone out, wouldn't you? I can't leave Abbie and Charlie in the house on their own. They'll have to come with us.'

Abbie and Charlie were not at all
pleased about that, and Dad soon
had a car full of grumpy people and
we went whizzing off to hospital.

Pete and I were silent.
I couldn't tell Dad we were trying
to catch Abbie and Charlie snogging,
could I? My head was throbbing like
a road drill.

We pulled up outside the hospital and Dad marched us to the desk. Two nurses looked at our flappy wings and began to giggle.

'I've brought a couple of damaged fairies for you to mend,' Dad announced in an icy voice.

'Let's start with your names,' giggled Nurse One.

'Real names, please,' demanded Nurse Two. 'Then you can go through to that cubicle and wait there. Sister will see to you in a few minutes.'

'Whose sister?' I asked, looking round. The nurses burst out laughing.

'She's not anyone's sister. She's called Sister because she's in charge of the nurses,' explained Nurse Two. 'You are funny.'

'I don't feel funny,' I mumbled.

Those nurses were a right pair, if you ask me. I mean, what a stupid name for a nurse. Why call her Sister? You might as well call her Auntie.

Poor Casper!

We went and sat in the cubicle, clutching tissues to our heads. Dad broke the gloomy silence by talking with lover-boy. 'I understand you want to be a doctor, Charlie. This will be very good experience for you.'

'Yes,' murmured Charlie, looking rather pale, not to mention worried.

Abbie was trying to hold Charlie's hand without anyone noticing. I nudged Pete and pointed silently. He began spluttering madly and Abbie quickly cottoned on that we'd seen. She snatched her hand away, but you should have seen how red she went! Like a fire engine, ON FIRE!

And that was when Sister appeared.

Eek! and Help! A battleship came steaming into the room and stood there with her hands stuck on her hips. Her eyes scoured us like a pair of scrubbing brushes.

Pete shrank back against the wall. 'Are you going to stitch us?' he croaked.

A smile creased Sister's face. She rubbed her hands together and aimed her pointy nose at us like some kind of missile. 'Oh, yes,' she answered brightly. 'I'm just going to get my sewing machine!'

SEWING MACHINE??

# AAARRRGH!

Pete and I looked at each other. This was absolutely desperate! It was definitely time for

It wasn't like that at all, of course. Sister wasn't a monster. In fact she was mega super *brilliantissimo*.

'I was only teasing about the sewing machine,' she laughed. 'Those cuts don't need stitches – I can superglue the pair of you.'

SUPERGLUE US?????

Dad was amazed. 'You can superglue them back together again?'

'Yes. It's a lot quicker. We use special medical superglue.'

I think everyone should be superglued. Except me.

'Can you superglue their mouths shut while you're at it?' asked Abbie, which I don't think was very kind at all. That sister of mine should keep *her* mouth shut, if you ask me. Sister just smiled and said she'd better take a look at the damage, and she carefully lifted off the tissues.

KERRFLOBBB!

That was the noise Charlie made when he fainted at the sight of blood and slumped to the floor! You should have heard the fuss Abbie made. She was on her knees in an instant, wringing her hands.

'Charlie! Charlie! Don't die, Charlie! I love you, Charlie!!'

Abbie bent over and began snogging him! She did! Of course, she said afterwards

that it was definitely NOT snogging, it was the Kiss of Life. But I know a snog when I see one, and in any case Charlie wasn't dying at all, unless it was from being smothered. Sister had to pull Abbie off the poor boy. (I was beginning to feel quite sorry for him. I mean, fancy having THAT CREATURE all over you.)

I'm with Casper on this one. Urrgh!

OH NO YOU DON'T!

The other nurses sorted Charlie out while Sister got to work on my head. In no time at all, she'd finished.

'There, that's got Plinky-Plonk sorted out. You can go back to your fairy toadstool now.' And she chuckled, but I thought she was being JOLLY RUDE! Fairy toadstool? Huh!

Pete's split forehead seemed to be taking her much longer than my cut had. Sister stopped and pulled a face.

'Oh dear, I seem to have got my fingers stuck to Winky-Wonk's head.'

And she had! Her fingers were superglued to Pete's forehead.

'Is it a big problem?' asked Dad.

'No, not really,' said Sister. 'See? I'm wearing a rubber glove so I can just wriggle my fingers out, like so. There!' And she pulled her hand away at last.

The three of us stared at Pete. He looked like a very sad fairy. A very, VERY sad fairy with a large rubber glove stuck to the front of his face.

Dad and I couldn't help it. Poor Pete looked so miserable, with his half-broken wings and the rubber glove flopping down over his big nose. We creased up and Sister was having hysterics too. She laughed like a tickled horse.

'I think Winky-Wonk's got a flinky-flonk on his face,' she neighed, before going off to find some special stuff you can use to get rid of superglue.

It was quite a while before we left the hospital. Pete went back to his house and we went back to ours. Charlie had gone home too, and Abbie was being a grump in the front room.

'I bet you were trying to see into my
room,' she said to me.

Mum smiled. 'Casper's right, Abbie. He's
been hurt. Go and get him a drink – and you
can make your father and me some coffee
while you're in the kitchen.'

Abbie's eyes narrowed to tiny slits, which meant she was thinking about all the horrible things she would like to do to us, especially me. But she couldn't because they were all AGAINST THE LAW! So she slunk off to the kitchen and brought me back a drink.

Sometimes I love my big sister!

My tongue's got the best superglue. Flies can't resist it!

HELP ME!

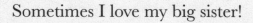

# OOOOo!!

That's the noise the cows in the playground made at school the other day. I know! Cows in the playground! *Big problemo!* How did that happen? I will tell you.

It began on Monday with Assembly. Miss Scratchitt, our head teacher, was giving us news about a school like ours. 'Only it's in Malawi. Does anyone know where Malawi is?'

Miss Scratchitt pointed at one of the youngest children. 'Thomas, where do you think Malawi is?'

The four-year-old pointed towards the windows. 'Over there,' he squeaked, and the older children laughed, especially Masher McNee, who snorted so hard some stuff came out of his nose.

'Perhaps *you* can tell us, Michael,' Miss Scratchitt suggested, looking pointedly at him. (Masher is his nickname because he's always mashing people.) Masher stopped snorting, frowned hard and finally said he didn't know.

Miss Scratchitt smiled triumphantly.

'Neither did Thomas,' she told him. 'Malawi is in Africa. It is a poor country. There are few schools there.'

'Hooray!' muttered Masher under his breath.

'Few children can read because they don't have books and there aren't enough teachers to teach them to read,' Miss Scratchitt told us. 'We are going to be twinned with a Malawian school. Their school is just like ours, and so are the children. They learn in classrooms and they like to play football and run around in the playground just like you, but they need our help. They need books, paper and pens, and money to pay for teachers. We can help them. Can any of you think of a way to help?'

Masher's hand waved furiously. Miss Scratchitt sighed, but she asked him anyway.

'Why don't we send *our* teachers to *their* school?!' Masher obviously thought this was his best idea ever.

Miss Scratchitt's eyes turned into slitty daggers. 'Michael, I know you want to help by getting rid of all our teachers here, but I can tell you now that if – IF – our teachers went to Malawi, they would instantly – INSTANTLY – be replaced by new teachers. Life here would carry on just as before.'

Masher and his gang gave a loud groan. I noticed Mr Butternut laughing into his hand. Sometimes I have no idea what my teacher is thinking about. He is a Man of Mystery.

I put up my hand. Miss Scratchitt nodded at me. 'Yes, Casper?'

'My great-gran used to live in Africa. She knows loads about it. She's always telling me stories.'

Miss Scratchitt perked up. 'Indeed? Perhaps your great-grandmother would like to come to our assembly one morning

and talk to all of us. That would
be splendid. What is your great-
grandmother's name?'

'Gee-Gee.'

Everyone fell about laughing. 'What's
so funny? She LIKES being called that.
It's double G, for great-gran.'

When I was a baby my mum called me Wee-Wee!

AND ALSO SHE LIKES HORSES. SO THERE!

More laughter. Pete was
sitting next to me, and now
he was waving his hand in
the air.

'It's true, Miss Scratchitt.
They shouldn't laugh,
because Casper's great-gran
is amazing and she's ninety
years old, and she's fought

with lions and stuff, and she
got swept over a waterfall, and
she's amazing, and her lunch
was stolen by an amazing
monkey, and there was a snake
in her bed, and she went on
a train for thousands of
miles just to go to school,
and she's amazing and –'

'Peter! Peter, please! You can stop now. We get the idea. We must certainly ask Casper's great-gran – Gee-Gee – to come to an assembly this week. I shall see to it.'

So that was what our assembly was all about. We are going to send our twin school in Malawi lots of books and paper, pencils and crayons, and stuff like that. We have been packing them into boxes, decorating them and writing letters. Mr Butternut said the children in Malawi will be very excited to get our letters.

I said they would be extra-excited to get mine because I had drawn a picture of Pete being squeezed by a python and his tongue sticking out.

'That's not very kind, Casper,' said Mr Butternut. 'I thought you two were friends.'

Pete shrugged. 'It's OK,' he said. 'I've drawn a picture of Casper being sat on by an elephant.'

Before school finished, Miss Scratchitt sent a note to all the classes saying that Gee-Gee had agreed to come into school at the end of the week to talk about her childhood in Africa.

Mr Butternut beamed at me. 'You must be very proud of your great-grandmother,' he said.

'Er, yes,' I muttered. Had he forgotten about the time Gee-Gee came to school, thrashed Masher McNee at football and almost caused a riot? I examined my teacher's face. He was giving nothing away. He was Mr Butternut, Man of Mystery. Definitely.

When I got home there was more news, from Mum this time.

'Gee-Gee rang and told me about your assembly. How exciting! She wants you to take some African things for her from the care home to school.'

I want to see this assembly!

'Right. Pete can come with me. I'll go and get him.' I opened the door to let myself out and there was Pete, about to come in. He looked pretty grim too.

'What's the matter?' I asked.

'Uncle Boring. That's the matter.

He's brought a huge cheese for us to eat after supper tonight and it stinks like a volcano erupting old socks.'

'*Molto terriblo!* Stinky cheese is yuck! Is he crazy or what?'

'I think he's crazy AND what,' Pete answered, with bulging eyes. His eyes often go like that, especially when he's staggered by some problem or other. 'I mean, WHAT is he? That is the question. He's not human. THAT is the answer. But I think I have a good way to get rid of him AND his stinky cheese.'

'Really?'

Uh-oh! Daft idea coming up!

'Yes. I'm going to send him to Malawi. I'm sure the children there will have lots of fun playing with him. They could poke him with sticks.'

'Why would they want to poke him with sticks?' I asked, rather confused.

'BECAUSE I WANT TO POKE HIM WITH A STICK EVERY TIME I SEE HIM!' Pete cried. 'Especially when he's got a big stinky cheese.'

'But how will you get him all the way to Africa, O Giant-Footed One?' I asked.

'I shall put a stamp on his head and shove him in the postbox, my Little Ginger Insect.'

'It will be very expensive to send Uncle Boring all the way to Africa,' I declared.

'In that case I shall put him in my

giant catapult and launch him through hyperspace. He will reach Africa in a millisecond.'

# SARAH SITTERBOUT'S BIT ABOUT STINKY CHEESE

Most cheeses are made from milk. The milk usually comes from cows, goats or sheep.

It's the mould that makes some cheeses smell. (It's quite OK to eat the mould in stinky cheese!) It won't make YOU stinky (but you might be stinky already)! Cheese has been found in Ancient Egyptian tombs - I bet that's really REALLY stinky!

We reached the care home and went in. It's easy to know which is Gee-Gee's room because she has a large, scary African mask hanging on the door. It's made of painted wood, has bits of grass for hair and real crocodile teeth in the mouth. SCARY, eh?!

Gee-Gee waved her hands at us as if she was shooing us away.

'Stay there and don't interrupt!' she snapped. 'I'm packing this trunk for your assembly.'

'There!' said Gee-Gee, shutting the lid with a bang. 'It's all yours. Take it away, boys!'

Phew! Did we struggle with Gee-Gee's trunk? Yes, we did. It was about the size of a small car.

'Good grief!' cried Pete. 'What's in it?'

'The whole of Africa,' I gasped. 'Come on!'

I don't know how we managed, but we got the trunk home. Then, the very next morning, we struggled into school with it and dumped it in the corner of the hall. All day long people wandered past and gazed at it, wondering what was inside.

What's in the trunk? Show me!

Friday arrived. Every class was in the hall for assembly, plus every teacher and every assistant. We all wanted to know what was in the trunk.

Gee-Gee was late. I was getting worried. I stared and stared at the door, wondering what had happened to her.

The double doors sprang back and in came Gee-Gee. She was nervous and kept looking guiltily behind her as if she was expecting to be arrested at any moment. That great-gran of mine is very peculiar sometimes!

Miss Scratchitt greeted Gee-Gee and led her to the front of the hall. The head teacher introduced her to everyone and explained that Gee-Gee used to live in Africa when she was growing up. Now she was going to tell us what it was like.

'I lived in Zambia,' Gee-Gee began. 'My parents had a farm there. We grew coffee and avocados.'

'Were there lots of wild animals?' asked another little one.

'Yes, lots. There were lions, zebras, elephants, ostriches, baboons, snakes, monkeys, giant ants, crocodiles, er –'

'Whales?' shouted one of the four-year-olds.

'Yes, of course, huge herds of whales. Whole junglefuls of them!' cried Gee-Gee, waving her arms violently to show how many whales there were. 'Whales living all over the farm!'

Gee-Gee turned to Miss Scratchitt. 'What on earth are you teaching these nincompoops?'

Miss Scratchitt pulled a face. 'They're very small children,' she murmured.

'And they've got very small brains, if you ask me,' huffed Gee-Gee. 'Now then, there were lots of dangerous animals. I was camping one night and there were lions growling around my tent. I went out and told them to stop because I was trying to sleep. They took no notice of me at all! So I biffed one on the nose. *BOFF!* Like that! Then they all ran away!

Gee-Gee is a very good storyteller!

'Another time, I had a fight with a snake. It was a big fat python. It reared up in front of me and opened its mouth to eat me. Do you know what I did? I gave it a HUGE uppercut! *SWOOSH-BANG!* Like that! Knocked the snake out completely. So I took it home and we ate it for supper.'

'URRRRGGHHH!' howled half the school. 'That is so YUCK!'

Gee-Gee was really getting into her stride now and went sailing on. 'Another time, I found a tiger in our kitchen and —'

Miss Scratchitt tapped Gee-Gee on her arm. 'I didn't think there were any tigers in Africa,' she said.

Gee-Gee took a step back and stared at Miss Scratchitt from top to toe and back again. 'IT WAS A TIGER!' Gee-Gee repeated. 'A TIGER IN MY KITCHEN AND IT WAS ARGUING WITH A KANGAROO OVER WHO WAS GOING TO EAT THE CHOCOLATE CAKE!'

Poor Miss Scratchitt! She hurriedly sat on the nearest chair. Mr Butternut's shoulders were heaving up and down. Mysterious, very mysterious.

'Now I am going to tell you about our neighbours at the farm,' Gee-Gee declared. 'They were not like your neighbours. There was a native village near us. Every Saturday they would put on their best costumes and dance. Their dancing was so exciting!'

I'm very good at dancing!

Gee-Gee threw open her trunk and everyone craned forward. She pulled out a tall drum, gave it a quick bang and handed it to a boy in the front row. Then she pulled out three more drums and handed them round. By this time the children in the front row were crowding round the drums and beginning to beat them.

# BUDUMM! BUDOOMM! BUDUMM! BUDOOMM!

Gee-Gee dived head first into the trunk, scrabbled around, and this time she brought out some masks. The children at the front, who were the youngest, of course – they always get the best seats, it's not fair – got even more excited. They held the masks in front of their faces and tried to scare each other. It worked too, because at least six

small children burst into tears, while the rest
were starting to shout and jump about to the
drums.

Finally, Gee-Gee reached into the trunk
and suddenly she was brandishing a spear! A
REAL ONE!

Miss Scratchitt was getting so worried she was hopping up and down, doing a dance of her own, her eyes glued to the spear. 'Um, I don't think . . . um, could you . . . um . . . would you mind? Oh dear, I feel quite faint!'

The drums were banging wildly and Gee-Gee was smiling and jabbing her spear at the ceiling. Half the school were now rising up and the hall floor trembled beneath a hundred pairs of stamping feet. Poor Miss Scratchitt had both hands over her face, watching the chaos through a gap in her fingers with one alarmed eye.

At that moment, Mrs Moppnot, the caretaker, rushed into the hall, screaming at aeroplane volume.

We looked out of the big hall windows.
It was true. Several cows were wandering
about aimlessly. Everyone looked at Miss
Scratchitt. She was the head. What was she
going to do about this? But Miss Scratchitt

did something quite useless: she dithered. And in that moment of dithering, my great-gran took charge.

'Follow me!' thundered Gee-Gee. 'I know how to deal with a few cows!' She flung open the doors to the playground and the WHOLE SCHOOL streamed out after her.

The cows took one look at the army of
small things with legs hurtling towards them,
not to mention the wild monster in black

waving a spear – and fled in all directions, as

Gee-Gee raced about yelling

# MoooOOOo!!

The teachers raced about, trying to make sure the cows kept away from their children. Miss Scratchitt raced about after Gee-Gee, asking her to kindly put her spear down before someone got hurt. And the cows raced about because they were cows.

This problem was going to need an army of superheroes. It was definitely time for

I wish that had happened! But it didn't. A big cattle truck pulled up outside school. Three men jumped out and came hurrying in.

They told everyone to keep well back. They rounded up the cows, then herded them out of the playground and on to the truck.

The excitement was over and we trudged back into the hall. On the way Pete asked me a question.

WHY DID *RATHER DIFFERENT* COW HAVE TWO TAILS?

BECAUSE THE FIRST ONE I DREW WAS TOO SHORT.

Pete told me I was an idiot. I told
him he was a bigger idiot than me.
Mr Horrible Hairy Face told us to
stop shouting at each other, so we
did. We shouted using sign language
instead. Ha ha! *Magnifico!*

One of the men came back to
the hall to tell us how the cows had
escaped. They had been on another

truck. Ahead
of them was an
old lady in an
electric wheelchair,
wobbling along
the pavement. (I
knew who that
was – Gee-Gee!) A
dog was running
along beside the
wheelchair and
barking.

'So it was all
started by that
old lady,' said the
truck driver. 'Who

would have thought a little old lady could create so many problems?' he added, scratching his head. Pete and I looked at each other and kept silent. No wonder Gee-Gee had looked so nervous when she came into the hall!

Miss Scratchitt suddenly called out to me. 'Casper? Where's your great-gran? She seems to have vanished!'

Was I surprised? NO!

'I expect she went home. She gets tired easily,' I said lamely.

'Well, she's left ALL her African things behind,' Miss Scratchitt pointed out. 'You'll have to take them home with you.'

Pete and I looked at each other

*Pete was right. Gee-Gee's amazing!*

again. That trunk! We were going to have to drag Africa all the way back to Gee-Gee's care home. If only we really WERE superheroes. Huh!

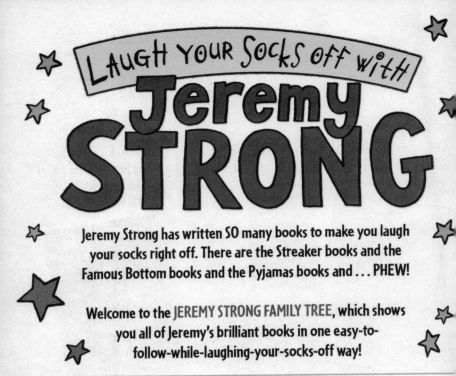

# LAUGH YOUR SOCKS OFF WITH Jeremy STRONG

Jeremy Strong has written SO many books to make you laugh your socks right off. There are the Streaker books and the Famous Bottom books and the Pyjamas books and . . . PHEW!

Welcome to the JEREMY STRONG FAMILY TREE, which shows you all of Jeremy's brilliant books in one easy-to-follow-while-laughing-your-socks-off way!

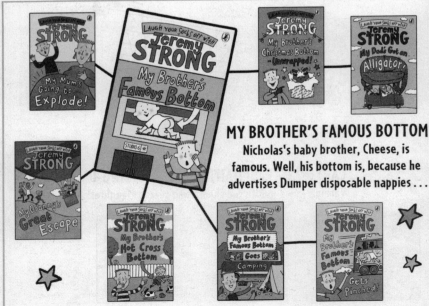

## MY BROTHER'S FAMOUS BOTTOM

Nicholas's baby brother, Cheese, is famous. Well, his bottom is, because he advertises Dumper disposable nappies . . .

# It all started with a Scarecrow

### Puffin is well over sixty years old.
Sounds ancient, doesn't it? But Puffin has never been
so lively. We're always on the lookout for the next big
idea, which is how it began all those years ago.

Penguin Books was a big idea from the mind of
a man called Allen Lane, who in 1935 invented
the quality paperback and changed the world.
**And from great Penguins, great Puffins grew,
changing the face of children's books forever.**

The first four Puffin Picture Books were hatched in 1940 and the
first Puffin story book featured a man with broomstick arms called
Worzel Gummidge. In 1967 Kaye Webb, Puffin Editor, started the
Puffin Club, promising to **'make children into readers'.**
She kept that promise and over 200,000 children became
devoted Puffineers through their quarterly installments of
*Puffin Post*, which is now back for a new generation.

Many years from now, we hope you'll look back and
remember Puffin with a smile. **No matter what your age
or what you're into, there's a Puffin for everyone.**
The possibilities are endless, but one thing is for sure:
whether it's a picture book or a paperback, a sticker book
or a hardback, **if it's got that little Puffin
on it – it's bound to be good.**